Ladybird Readers

The
Peter Rabbit
Club

Series Editor: Sorrel Pitts
Text adapted by Sorrel Pitts

LADYBIRD BOOKS

UK | USA | Canada | Ireland | Australia
India | New Zealand | South Africa

Ladybird Books is part of the Penguin Random House group of companies
whose addresses can be found at global.penguinrandomhouse.com.
www.penguin.co.uk   www.puffin.co.uk   www.ladybird.co.uk

First published 2017
001

Printed in China

A CIP catalogue record for this book is available from the British Library

ISBN: 978-0-241-29811-4

All correspondence to:
Ladybird Books
Penguin Random House Children's
80 Strand, London WC2R 0RL

Ladybird Readers

The Peter Rabbit Club

Based on the
Peter Rabbit™ TV series

Picture words

Benjamin

Peter

Lily

Mr. Tod

Old Brown

Tommy Brock

worms

wheelbarrow

rabbit hole

string

pull

"Let's start a club!" said
Peter. "We can do things
together in our club."

"We can have a lot
of fun in our club,"
said Lily.

"Yes!" said Benjamin.
"I am hungry! Let's
find some lunch."

Mr. Tod, Old Brown,
and Tommy Brock
were hungry, too.

"Let's catch the rabbits," said Mr. Tod. "Then, we can have rabbit for our lunch!"

"I want worms with my rabbit," said Tommy Brock. "I love worms."

The rabbits went to
Mr. McGregor's garden
for some lunch.
The rabbits heard a noise.

"Who's that?" said Peter.
"Let's go! This is not
our garden!"

It was Mr. Tod.

"I'm hungry,
and I want
my lunch!"
he said.

The rabbits ran to their rabbit hole.

"You can't go in this hole," said Tommy Brock.

"Come on!" Peter said.
"Let's go!"

They ran to the
garden wall.

"No! You can't go," said
Old Brown.

The rabbits could not leave
Mr. McGregor's garden!

"I'm hungry, and
I want my lunch!"
Mr. Tod said.

The rabbits wanted
to leave the garden.
They did not want
to be Mr. Tod's lunch!

Peter had a plan. He found a worm, and took it to Tommy Brock. Tommy Brock loved worms!

"Here is a worm for you," he said.

Then, he ran from
Tommy Brock.

"Catch that rabbit!"
called Mr. Tod.

Then, Mr. Tod and Tommy
Brock ran after Peter Rabbit.

"I want rabbit for my lunch,
too!" said Old Brown.

"Here comes Peter!"
said Lily and Benjamin.

"Stop!" said Peter.
"Stop them under the
wheelbarrow!"

Lily got some string.

Peter ran under the wheelbarrow. Then, he ran into the garden.

"Catch that rabbit!"
said Mr. Tod.

Mr. Tod, Tommy Brock, and Old Brown ran after Peter. They went under the wheelbarrow.

"Stop them with the string!" said Peter.

Lily pulled the string.

Mr. Tod, Tommy Brock, and Old Brown were under the wheelbarrow!

The rabbits ran from
Mr. McGregor's garden.
Then, they ate some lunch.

"That was fun!" said Peter.

"This is a good club!" said Benjamin.

"We are The Peter Rabbit Club!" said Lily.

Activities

The key below describes the skills practiced in each activity.

 Spelling and writing

 Reading

 Speaking

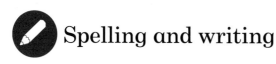 Critical thinking

Preparation for the Cambridge Young Learners Exams

1 **Look and read. Circle *Yes, it is* or *No, it isn't*.**

1  Is this Peter Rabbit?
a Yes, it is. **b** No, it isn't.

2  Is this Tommy Brock?
a Yes, it is. **b** No, it isn't.

3  Is this Lily?
a Yes, it is. **b** No, it isn't.

4  Is this Old Brown?
a Yes, it is. **b** No, it isn't.

5  Is this Mr. Tod?
a Yes, it is. **b** No, it isn't.

2 **Look at the letters. Write the words.**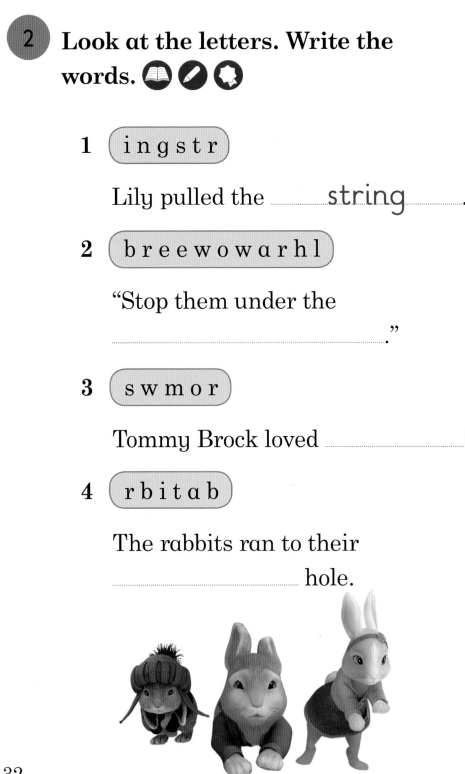

1 (i n g s t r)

Lily pulled the _____ string _____.

2 (b r e e w o w a r h l)

"Stop them under the

_____."

3 (s w m o r)

Tommy Brock loved _____!

4 (r b i t a b)

The rabbits ran to their

_____ hole.

32

3 **Look and read. Circle the correct words.**

1 "Let's start a **garden,**" / **club,**" said Peter.

2 "We can do things **together** / **there** in our club," said Peter.

3 "We can have a lot of **worms** / **fun** in our club," said Lily.

4 "Yes!" said Benjamin. "I am **hungry!**" / **tired!**"

5 Let's find some **string,**" / **lunch,**" said Benjamin.

4 **Who says this? Write the correct names on the lines.** 📖 ✏️ ⬡

| Peter | Mr. Tod | Tommy Brock | Old Brown |

1 "Let's start a club!" _____Peter_____

2 "Let's go! This is not our garden!" _____

3 "I'm hungry, and I want my lunch!" _____

4 "You can't go in this hole." _____

5 "No! You can't go!" _____

6 "Let's catch the rabbits." _____

5 Complete the sentences.
Write a—d. 📖

1 Mr. Tod, Old Brown, and
Tommy Brock were ....b........

2 "Let's catch the ....

3 "Then, we can have ....

4 "I want worms with ....

> **a** rabbit for our lunch!"
>
> **b** hungry.
>
> **c** my rabbit," said Tommy Brock.
>
> **d** rabbits," said Mr. Tod.

The rabbits went to
Mr. McGregor's garden
for some lunch.
The rabbits heard a noise.

"Who's that?" said Peter.
"Let's go! This is not
our garden!"

The rabbits went to Mr. McGregor's

¹ **garden** for some lunch. The

rabbits heard a ² _____.

"Who's ³ _____?" said Peter.

"Let's ⁴ _____!

⁵ _____ is not our garden!"

7 **Find the words.**

hungry
hole
lunch
rabbit
worms

apshungryindlunchkmewormsfrirabbitjkaholedra

8 Talk about the two pictures with a friend. How are they different? Use the words in the box. ◯

a

The rabbits went to Mr. McGregor's garden for some lunch. The rabbits heard a noise.

"Who's that?" said Peter. "Let's go! This is not our garden!"

b

The rabbits ran to their rabbit hole.

"You can't go in this hole," said Tommy Brock.

standing   eating   frightened
Tommy Brock   garden   running

In picture a, the rabbits are standing.

In picture b, the rabbits are running.

9 **Circle the correct words.** 📖 ✏️

1 (**What**)/ **Why** did Peter want to start?

2 **What / Why** did Peter want to start a club?

3 **What / Where** did Lily want to have in their club?

4 **What / Where** did the rabbits go for lunch?

5 **What / Why** did Benjamin call the club at the end?

10 Look and read. Write the correct names in the boxes. 📖 ✏️ ❓

Lily   Tommy Brock   Old Brown

Benjamin   Mr. Tod   Peter

In The Peter Rabbit Club	Not in The Peter Rabbit Club
Lily	

Peter had a plan. He found a worm, and took it to Tommy Brock. Tommy Brock loved worms!

"Here is a worm for you," he said.

18

Then, he ran from Tommy Brock.

19

1 Peter **(find)** ___found___ a worm.

2 Peter **(take)** _____ the worm to Tommy Brock.

3 Peter **(give)** _____ the worm to Tommy Brock.

4 Then, Peter **(run)** _____ from Tommy Brock.

5 Peter **(find)** _____ his friends.

12 **Look, match, and write the words.**

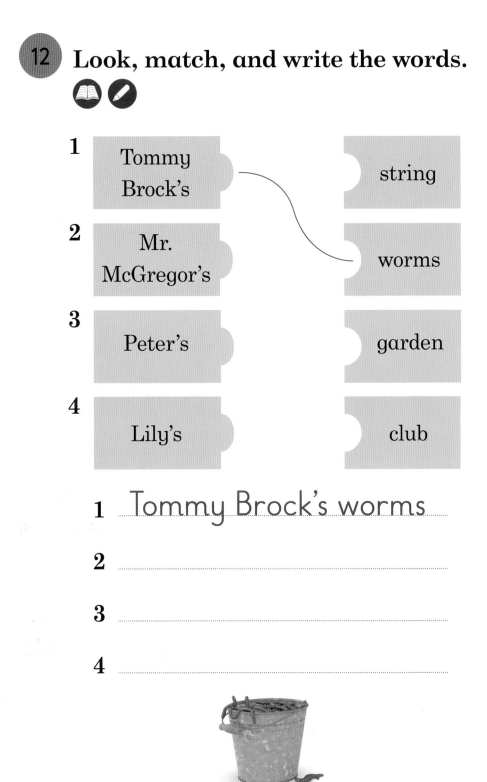

1 Tommy Brock's — string

2 Mr. McGregor's — worms

3 Peter's — garden

4 Lily's — club

1 Tommy Brock's worms

2 ....

3 ....

4 ....

13 Do the crossword.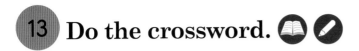

¹s	t	r	i	n	²g

³w

⁴r

Across

1 Lily pulled this.

3 Peter ran under this.

4 Mr. Tod, Tommy Brock, and Old Brown wanted to eat these.

Down

2 The rabbits went to Mr. McGregor's . . .

3 Peter found a . . . for Tommy Brock.

14 Read the questions. Write answers using words in the box.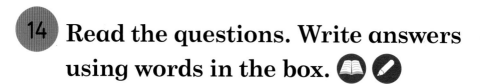

> Old Brown
> under
> garden
> string

1 Who flew after Peter?

  Old Brown flew after Peter.

2 What did Lily get?

  Lily got some _____.

3 Where did Peter run?

  Peter ran _____ the wheelbarrow.

4 Where did the rabbits run from?

  The rabbits ran from Mr. McGregor's

_____.

15 Write *after*, *under*, or *into*.

1 "Stop!" said Peter. "Stop them
        _____under_____ the wheelbarrow!"

2 Mr. Tod, Tommy Brock, and Old
   Brown ran _____ Peter.

3 Peter ran _____ the
   wheelbarrow.

4 Then, he ran _____
   the garden.

16 Work with a friend. You are Tommy Brock. Your friend is Mr. Tod. Ask and answer questions.

1 Do you have some rabbits, Mr. Tod?

No, I do not!

2 Did you catch Peter?

3 Are you happy under this wheelbarrow?

17 **Order the story. Write 1—5.** 📖

_____ Mr. Tod, Tommy Brock, and Old Brown ran after Peter.

__1__ Peter and his friends started The Peter Rabbit Club.

_____ Mr. Tod wanted to catch the rabbits, and eat them.

_____ Peter and his friends went to Mr. McGregor's garden.

_____ Lily got some string and stopped them.

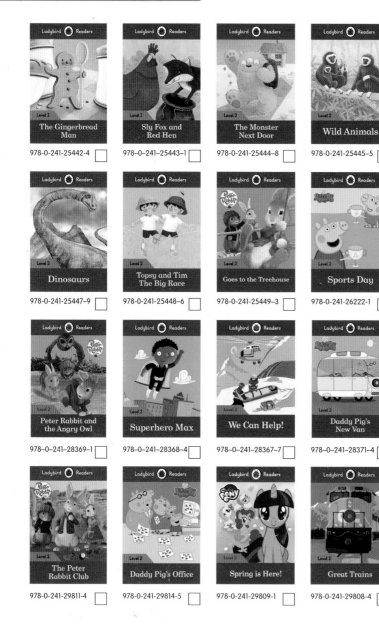

The Gingerbread Man	**Sly Fox and Red Hen**	**The Monster Next Door**	**Wild Animals**	**Little Red Riding Hood**
978-0-241-25442-4	978-0-241-25443-1	978-0-241-25444-8	978-0-241-25445-5	978-0-241-25446-2
Dinosaurs	**Topsy and Tim The Big Race**	**Goes to the Treehouse**	**Sports Day**	**Going on a Picnic**
978-0-241-25447-9	978-0-241-25448-6	978-0-241-25449-3	978-0-241-26222-1	978-0-241-26221-4
Peter Rabbit and the Angry Owl	**Superhero Max**	**We Can Help!**	**Daddy Pig's New Van**	**School Trip**
978-0-241-28369-1	978-0-241-28368-4	978-0-241-28367-7	978-0-241-28371-4	978-0-241-28372-1
The Peter Rabbit Club	**Daddy Pig's Office**	**Spring is Here!**	**Great Trains**	**Hungry Animals**
978-0-241-29811-4	978-0-241-29814-5	978-0-241-29809-1	978-0-241-29808-4	978-0-241-29844-2

Now you're ready for Level 3!